A Gift For:

_____

From:

_____

THE
SHEPHERDS'
PRAYER

A Christmas Novel

RICHARD M. BARRY

RM BARRY
PUBLICATIONS

Published by RM Barry Publications, Englewood, Colorado

Some scripture quotations are taken from the King James Version of the Bible. Public domain.

Some scripture quotations are taken from the American Standard Version of the Bible. Public domain.

Some scripture quotations are taken from the New American Standard Bible® (NASB), Copyright © 1960, 1962, 1963, 1968, 1971, 1972, 1973, 1975, 1977, 1995 by The Lockman Foundation. Used by permission. (www.lockman.org)

Some scripture quotations are taken from the Amplified® Bible, Copyright © 1954, 1958, 1962, 1965, 1987 by The Lockman Foundation. Used by permission. (www.lockman.org)

Some scripture quotations are taken from The Holy Bible, New Living Translation, Copyright © 1996. Used by permission of Tyndale House Publishers, Inc., Wheaton, Illinois 60189. All rights reserved.

For information or bulk orders:
RM Barry Publications
P.O. Box 3528
Littleton, CO 80161-3528
888-209-0510
www.ShepherdsPrayer.com

Jacket Design by The DesignWorks Group, Sisters, Oregon.

ISBN: 0-9767290-5-9

Printed in the United States of America

This book is dedicated to the shepherds of Bethlehem, who, I believe, may be some of the greatest unsung heroes in the Bible.

THE
SHEPHERDS'
PRAYER

PROLOGUE

Lydia struggled to stay in the saddle as the frantic horse dodged briar-laden bushes and jumped over other obstacles in its path. She tried to see if the killers were chasing her, but turning her head to look almost made her lose her balance as the horse stumbled and lurched through the dark, inhospitable Judean wilderness. She tightened her grip on the baby in her arms.

Her mind reeled. The screams of horrified mothers and fathers still echoed in her ears, as did the snuffed-out cries of their slain children. The terrible scene flashed through her memory over and over. She struggled to comprehend what was happening back in the peaceful little village of Bethlehem where she lived.

Every motherly instinct she had told her that her only chance to escape with her son's life was to ride as fast and as far as she could. So she jabbed her heels into the horse's side, urging the poor animal to continue the frenzied pace, clinging with all her strength to her baby with one arm, and to the saddle with the other.

The horse panted heavily, steamy mist pouring from its flared nostrils. The desert brush tore at Lydia's nightclothes and cut into her skin as the horse raced over the unfamiliar terrain.

She had never ridden a horse before, only donkeys, and she made no attempt to guide it. The night was dark, so she couldn't see where she was going anyway. All she knew was that Bethlehem and the cries of her neighbors were behind her.

Eventually the exhausted horse slowed to an unsteady trot as it struggled in vain to catch its breath. Lydia was finally able to turn to see if she was being pursued, but it was too dark to see anything. Then the horse staggered sideways down a steep slope as Lydia struggled to hang on. The horse finally collapsed onto the rocky bottom of a dry creek bed. Lydia's body slammed to the ground, still gripping the saddle. A sharp pain shot up her leg, searing her mind with agony, and she immediately slipped out of consciousness.

When she woke again, Lydia thought for a moment she had been asleep in her bed, and it had all been a terrible dream. But as she slowly became aware of her surroundings, she realized this was no dream. Her skin was numb from the cold, and she couldn't feel her leg which was trapped under the fallen animal, now lifeless and still. She lay for a moment under the dark, moonless sky, gradually trying to make sense of her predicament, and she understood she was dying. In her condition, she would not survive the night.

"My baby!" She was suddenly stricken with panic as she remembered her infant son. She reached out blindly into the darkness for him. He was next to her, still wrapped tightly in the lambskin. Lydia pulled a corner of the blanket away from his face, and breathed a deep sigh of relief when she heard his cry. He seemed to be unharmed, and she murmured a prayer of thanks to God. Then she began to weep at the thought that he, too, might succumb to the elements before anyone would find them.

With her last bit of strength, Lydia pulled the infant close to her breast to shield him from the wind and the biting desert cold. Caressing him, she whispered, "My sweet baby." Then she prayed through her tears, "Oh Lord, I give my child to you. Use him as you will, but please let him live. Please, Lord … deliver my son to safety."

1
CHAPTER

$\mathcal{A}$nam sat at the family gathering wishing he could be more cheerful, but the occasion only served to remind him, once again, that he did not fit in. His father, Micah, sat at the head of the table. Anam noticed a gleam in his eye as Micah looked with pride upon his large family assembled there. They were a handsome lot. His sons had grown tall and strong. All but the youngest had taken wives, who were with them, along with his many grandchildren.

They were celebrating because Anam's younger brother, sixteen-year-old John, was now engaged to be married too. Micah had arranged the marriage with a business associate of his. The union of his son with the man's fourteen-year-old daughter would enlarge the profits of both merchants.

That left Anam as the only single man at the table, though he was nearly thirty, a realization that made him feel more out of place than usual. He was not related to the others by blood, but Micah's sons treated him like a brother. And Micah had always cared for him like one of his own. Yet this event reminded him once again of the sad fact that he did not really belong.

The eldest son, Aaron, turned to his white-bearded father. "Are you going to bestow a blessing upon the boy?" He winked at his youngest brother. "He is to be married soon, so he will need all the help he can get!"

The brothers roared with laughter. Their wives rolled their eyes and smiled demurely, the way women were expected to. The children giggled along with the adults, though they didn't understand the joke. Anam didn't think it was very funny, but he loved hearing the laughter of children. They always seemed to have such light hearts that laughter came naturally for them. In a way he was envious of them.

Micah stood from his position at the head of the table.

His beloved wife, Miriam, had died four years earlier, and he insisted that her seat next to his remain vacant as a permanent tribute and reminder of her life. His sons had urged him to remarry, but the old man had no interest in any other woman. The patriarch fixed his gaze upon his family, then raised his eyes toward heaven. "We beseech ye, oh Yahweh, maker of heaven and earth, to bestow thy blessings upon John. Bless the union he will enter into with the fruit of children and the goodness of heaven."

They all bowed their heads and recited a solemn "Amen" in perfect unison.

The women went to work at once, carrying heaping platters of food to the large wooden table. The scent of fresh-baked bread and roasted meats filled the air. Micah had ordered the fatted calf slaughtered, and they feasted on it along with lamb, cooked vegetables, bread, and wine.

Anam was pleased that his brother would now be married and start a family. He wished John nothing but happiness. But his mood was gloomy as he ate quietly and kept to himself, in stark contrast to the brothers, who were their usual boisterous selves. Jacob, the second-oldest brother, finished his third glass of wine and poured himself another. His wife whispered something to him. Jacob shook his head dismissively, then turned toward Anam. "You are the luckiest amongst us, my good man."

Confused, Anam quietly said, "How do you mean?"

"You have no wife nagging you about how much you drink!" He slapped Anam on the back as his brothers laughed.

"I'll drink to that," Aaron said.

From across the table, Anam caught the look on his compassionate father's face, as Micah locked eyes with his adopted son. The old man's deep wrinkles around his eyes spoke volumes. He obviously felt Anam's pain, but would not embarrass him by addressing it here at the table. It helped Anam to get through the rest of the dinner without punching one of his brothers. They had no idea that their good-natured barbs were so hurtful.

After dinner, Anam slipped away from the family and wandered out into the fields. The sun was setting behind the hills in the distance. He pulled his cloak more tightly around his neck against the evening chill. "You are the living God," he said aloud into the gathering darkness. "I need guidance. This cannot be my lot for the rest of my life. There must be more. Please show me."

He listened to the wind as it softly fluttered among the trees. A faint whisper came to his ear. Whether or not it was audible, he could not tell. Yet it was a voice … and it told him the time had come to go to Micah, his father, and pour out his heart.

2
CHAPTER

The night wore on and the festivities died down. The children fell asleep first, followed soon by their fathers (helped by too much wine), who were dutifully joined by their wives after they cleaned up following the meal.

Anam, however, had no intention of going to sleep yet. He felt the hand of God upon his shoulder, urging him to speak with his father openly—man to man. There was no turning back now. Anam gathered up his courage and went back inside the house. The sweet aroma of the evening's feast still lingered in the air as he quietly made his way to his father's private quarters, careful not to wake any of the others.

A faint light flickered from beneath the closed door. *He must be up reading. Perhaps it is best not to disturb him,* Anam told himself. He turned to walk away, but something stopped him. *No! I must do this,* he resolved.

He knocked lightly on the door.

After a shuffling of footsteps, Micah appeared in the doorway. "Anam," he said, "I thought you were in bed like the others."

"I could not sleep, Father."

Micah ushered him inside and closed the door. "Now," he said, "tell me what is bothering you."

How does he know something is bothering me? It must show on my face. I swear that man can see right through me sometimes! Anam's eyes turned toward the large parchment scrolls carefully laid out on the table next to Micah's bed, illuminated by a dim lantern. "I see that you were reading from the sacred Scriptures, Father. I am sorry for disturbing you."

The old man smiled and rested his weary bones in a chair

next to his bed. "To tell you the truth, I needed the break. What I was reading was … well, let's say, very disturbing."

Though he wanted to get right to his question, Anam found Micah's statement riveting. "Is it from the Pentateuch?" he asked, referring to the portion of Holy Writ he was most familiar with.

"No, it is from the inspired utterances of the prophet Isaiah."

Anam nodded when he heard the name. He was certainly familiar with the great prophet, but embarrassed to admit he did not know all of his writings. "He was a great man of God who lived hundreds of years ago, is that not correct?"

The old man nodded. "Yes, but his words seem to speak clearly to our own day. The passage I just read tells of a mysterious figure—a servant who will come and give his life to save his people."

Anam vaguely recalled hearing of this passage before, but he wanted to know more. "How can a servant save anyone?" he asked, perplexed.

"I do not know, my son. But Isaiah says that this servant will be despised by men, reviled. He will suffer much, but his suffering will not be in vain. In fact, through his suffering God will heal the nations, and this servant will be glorified."

"The prophet has indeed given us a strange story, Father. What does it mean?"

Micah sighed deeply. "I wish I had the answer. I do not fully understand it myself. But I think what he is trying to tell us is that we must look at suffering in a different way; we must see it from God's perspective rather than just man's. This was written in the distant past, but even now our people suffer greatly under the oppression of the Romans. That makes me wonder if Isaiah was speaking to us today."

There was silence for a moment as Anam absorbed his father's words.

Micah stood and carefully rolled up the parchment scrolls. After kissing them, he reverently placed them on the shelf in the corner of the room. Then he patted Anam on the shoulder, saying, "But I know you did not come here to discuss prophecy. So tell me, what is on your mind?"

Anam cleared his throat. "Please understand that I mean no disrespect by this question. You have been a kind and loving father to me all of my life, and I thank God every day for you. But ..."

Micah's old eyes looked upon him with pity. "But you want to know about the circumstances of your birth. You want to know where you came from."

Bowing his head, Anam whispered, "Yes."

"I knew this day would come. In fact, it is to your credit that it took so many years before you finally came to me and asked. You have always been most respectful." Micah sat again in the chair beside his bed. "Now I will tell you all that I know."

Anam sat at his father's feet and felt his throat tighten as he listened to the story he had always wanted to hear, but never dared ask about.

"It was many years ago … it seems like yesterday, but it's been almost thirty years now. I was traveling alone—not a wise thing for a merchant to do, but in my younger years I took chances. I was on my way home from a successful trading mission in Jerusalem. It was early in the morning, and my donkey was heavily laden with merchandise I had purchased in the great city. I was filled with happy thoughts of returning home, where I knew my beloved wife Miriam would be waiting for me. I also anticipated the money I could make with all the fine products I had shrewdly negotiated for.

"Then, before me on the road, I came across something that would change my life forever. From a dry creek bed off to the side of the road, I thought I heard something, a wailing sort of sound. I stopped dead in my tracks. My donkey began braying and kicking. Something had frightened him. The first thought that crossed my mind was that there were thieves lying in wait. They would pounce upon me and steal my goods. In fear of my life, I unsheathed my dagger and moved cautiously toward the edge of the creek bed to take a closer look.

"I cannot tell you how astonished I was when, rather than bandits, I saw a Roman soldier's horse toppled over on its side. It was dead, having apparently been ridden to exhaustion. Next to the animal, wrapped in a lambskin blanket, was an infant. The child was crying, and I picked him up to comfort him."

Anam had been listening intently. He swallowed hard as the reality of Micah's words sunk in. "The child was me?"

"Yes."

"I was all alone?"

Micah stroked his long white beard, a gesture Anam knew he did when something was bothering him.

"There was a woman. She lay pinned beneath the dead horse. With all my strength I managed to pull her out from under the carcass. But I was too late. She also was dead. That woman, I can only presume, must have been your mother."

A tear clouded Anam's vision as he waited for the old man to continue.

"The scene was a mystery to me. I couldn't understand why a woman would be riding a horse that—it was obvious from the saddle and other gear—belonged to a Roman soldier. The woman was wearing only a nightdress, her feet were bare, and it was very cold at night that time of year. She must have died from her injuries and from exposure to the cold. Fortunately for the baby … I mean you … you were tightly wrapped in the blanket and shielded from the cold and wind by the woman's tight embrace.

"I laid her body across my donkey, leaving most of my merchandise by the side of the road, and took her back to our town for a proper burial. Of course, I took the baby with me too, carrying you in my arms the remainder of the trip.

"Ah, you were a fine-looking child, Anam, and when I held you, you stopped crying. I wanted to consider you as my own child from that very first day, as did Miriam when I showed you to her. However, when we took you to the elders at the synagogue, they noted that you had already been circumcised. According to the laws of our people, given to us by the Most High, that meant you were a Jew and had already been given a name on the day of your circumcision. It would dishonor your parents, alive or dead, to give you another name. That is why we deemed it necessary to call you Anam, which literally means 'no-name.' It fulfilled the letter of the law."

Anam sighed deeply. He knew all too well the meaning of his name. For him it had been an endless source of shame for as long as he could remember.

Micah paused and leaned forward from his chair, placing his hand on Anam's shoulder with the same compassionate look in his eyes Anam had seen earlier at the dinner table. Then Micah sat back and continued his story. "The elders told me that it was my duty to try to find your family and return you to them. But the circumstances of your birth were shrouded in mystery. The only clue I had, in fact, was the lambskin blanket you were wrapped in when I found you."

Anam cocked his head. "How could a blanket tell you anything about who I was?"

Micah nodded as if to confirm a long-held belief. "The time has come for you to see as well as to hear."

The old man ambled over to an oblong wooden chest that lay at the foot of his bed. Ever since he was a child, Anam had wondered what was inside, but his father always kept it under lock and key. The aged hinges groaned in protest as Micah opened the lid. The musty smell of things stored away for many years permeated the room. Micah carefully retrieved a lambskin blanket from deep within the chest and handed it to Anam.

"It is beautiful," he said as his fingers caressed the soft, white wool.

"Go on," said Micah. "Read the inscription."

Embedded with ink into the tanned hide were these words, which Anam read aloud: "Glory to God in the highest heaven, and peace on earth to men of good will, through Jesus Christ, who was born of Mary in a stable in Bethlehem and who, wrapped in swaddling clothes, was in a manger, he who is the Savior of the world."

Micah smiled. "Yes, yes. I remember those words, each and every one of them, as if I had just read them yesterday. They have remained with me, close to my heart, all these many years, and I have often pondered their meaning."

Anam stood, his heart pounding with excitement. "Father, I do not understand what these words mean. Who is this Jesus? And Mary? I do not know of these people. Are they my relatives?"

Micah shook his head. "I tried to find out the answers, but it has remained a mystery to this day. I want you to know, however, that this blanket is rightfully your property. I have faithfully preserved it for you, for this very day, and now I want you to keep it."

Tears welled up in the young man's eyes as he hugged the blanket close to his body. It was a connection to his past, the only link in fact, and it stirred within him a passion to know more.

"You said this blanket was your only clue, Father. Did it lead you any closer to the truth?"

Micah sat in his chair again and sighed heavily, "The truth was indeed what I was seeking. With the blessing of our town's elders, I set out back up the road the same way I had come, in hopes of finding your family. When I came to Bethlehem, I heard of a terrible evil that had befallen that place. It seems that the king had received information that a child had been born who would someday present a challenge to his throne. So he ordered all the male infants in that town to be slaughtered. The killing was horrific; the grief it caused, indescribable.

"I surmised that your mother must have fled from the town to save you from a certain and cruel death. In her flight, she happened upon a horse that belonged to one of Herod's soldiers. She urged the horse on as fast and as far as it would go, until it finally collapsed in the creek bed where I found you.

"I hoped this great tragedy would lead me to your family. My heart rejoiced in thinking how happy they would be to have you back. But it was not to be. The more I asked about this mystery child I had found, the more hostile the people became toward me. They were angry and suspicious of me. Before long, I was met with a wall of silence as one by one they refused to speak with me. Realizing the futility of my quest, I returned home. And from that day on, you became my son."

Hearing this story now for the first time, nearly three decades after it had occurred, caused all sorts of emotions to flood Anam's being. Micah's incredible tale prompted more questions than answers. And who was this mysterious Jesus that the lambskin blanket spoke of? He was determined to find out.

"Father, I know what I must do. I shall travel to Bethlehem myself and seek out answers." He then bowed his head in deference to the kindly old man who loved him so much. "That is, sir, with your blessing."

"Come here," Micah said, gesturing Anam to his side. He placed his hands on the young man's head and uttered a prayer over him. Anam closed his eyes as he listened intently to every word. Then Micah dismissed him and sent him on his way, saying, "May the God of Abraham, Isaac, and Jacob be with you, my son. And may the living God who alone guards all truth guide your every footstep."

CHAPTER

Anam had traveled with his father on many trading journeys. Once they had sojourned as far north as the land of Lebanon. Ah, how he recalled the magnificent cedars, tall and majestic still, as in the days of old. But this trip was much different. It was not for commerce, or any sort of monetary gain. In fact, he felt almost like a beggar, as he carried with him only those meager provisions he could fit in the sack he had tied to the end of a thick stick with a leather thong.

Another major difference from his previous trips was that this time he was alone. This was by choice. He did not want a companion, as he considered this a personal quest—something that he needed to do all by himself. God would be with him, and that would be enough.

The road he chose to take was not well traveled. Yes, it would be more dangerous than the more popular roads, with their merchant caravans, military patrols, and everyday foot traffic, but that was fine by him. He needed time to think, and to pray. As far back as Anam could remember, these things always came to him more powerfully in solitude.

Though it was late in the year, the sun beat down upon his face relentlessly throughout the midday hours, and he occasionally wiped his brow with the sleeve of his tunic to keep the stinging perspiration out of his eyes. As dusk approached, Anam picked up his pace and walked more briskly along the dirt path, hoping to reach the inn his father had told him about before the sun set behind the gently sloping hills in the distance.

He came to a bend in the road. *Surely the inn must be up ahead*, he thought to himself. From the directions he had been given, he knew he was close. But as his eyes peered into the twilight, only more road lay ahead of him. That was okay; he simply returned his thoughts to where they had been all day. He kept asking God, *What exactly is it that*

I'm searching for? Is a name really all that important? Will it change who I truly am? Can I be a righteous man even without a family heritage? As always, Anam found himself with more questions than answers.

As darkness continued to envelop the road, he realized that he would not reach the inn before nightfall. Traveling on a dark road was not wise. Though he carried few possessions, alone and unarmed he could easily fall prey to bandits who might just as well kill him for not providing anything for them to steal.

Anam took refuge under a large, slightly bent willow tree at the far edge of a farmer's field. He placed his provisions on the ground and lay on his back.

It was so quiet out here. Back home he could always hear his father's snoring, the neighbors arguing, or one of his brothers stumbling toward the outhouse in the middle of the night. There was none of that now. He was alone with his thoughts.

Far above him, the vault of God's heaven presented itself to his eyes. Anam recalled the words of David: *The heavens declare the glory of God; and the firmament showeth His handiwork.* Wise words indeed. He would keep them, along with the other sacred writings, close to his heart, just as his father had always instructed him.

Without a doubt, the stars were beautiful tonight, each one shining brightly against the backdrop of velvety blackness. *What a magnificent display of Yahweh's power*, he thought. *Why would the ruler of the universe, the One who spoke all this creative wonder into existence, care about a humble man like me? A man without a name.*

Yet Anam knew there was a place for him in this world, a purpose for his life. If only he could find it.

He fell asleep counting the multitude of stars, trying to comprehend so much that was beyond his reach.

The next morning, the crowing of a barnyard cock awoke Anam from his slumber. He rubbed his eyes and laughed when he heard his stomach rumbling. How long had it been since he had last eaten? Almost a full day, save for some small loaves he had eaten during yesterday's walk. He stretched, gathered up his belongings, and made his way across the field toward the road. *How different everything looks in the daylight*, he mused. The field, now dappled in sunshine, seemed much more pleasant. As fascinated as he was by the stars, Anam loved the morning. It was his favorite time of day and always gave him a renewed sense of what was possible.

Within a mile, the little-used road Anam had walked all day yesterday linked up with the more traveled road that headed directly into Bethlehem. A man with a donkey crossed his path. "Peace, friend," Anam said. The man just nodded and kept going. Anam waved to farmers he passed working their fields. They paid him little attention. He saw women carrying water back from the local well to their families, but he knew better than to greet them. Conversing with women who were not kin or close acquaintances could be scandalous, and Anam wasn't looking for trouble—just answers.

Finally, he entered the town of Bethlehem. It was much smaller than he had expected, basically just a few small shops including a blacksmith, some stables, a tavern, and an inn. With his stomach growling loudly, Anam decided to stop first at the tavern for some food.

A young man greeted him when he walked through the door. The smell of freshly baked bread filled the air. His mouth watering, Anam told the man he would like some breakfast. "Take a seat over there," the young man instructed, pointing to a small table and two chairs, "and I will bring you food."

Anam sat down and placed the sack with his belongings next to him on the floor. A few minutes later the young man brought him bread, water, and a bowl of steamed vegetables. He placed the food on the table, along with two plates. "Mind if I join you?" he asked. "I haven't eaten yet myself."

With a warm smile, Anam said, "Please, friend, sit and eat. I could use the company." He extended his hand. "My name is Anam."

Shaking his hand briefly, the young man's eyes held that same questioning look people had always had when Anam revealed his very uncommon and somewhat mysterious name. "I'm Reuben. Do you have family here in Bethlehem?"

Anam chewed his food and drank some water. He could feel his strength returning as the nourishment worked its way through his body. "Actually, the point of my visit is to find out about my family."

Reuben stared at Anam with an inquisitive look on his face and stopped chewing for a moment.

As Anam finished his first piece of bread and started his second, he explained his story, concluding by telling the young man about the inscription on the lambskin blanket. "In fact," he said with a smile, "I have it with me." He reached into the sack at his feet and with great care retrieved his treasured possession. "Read it for yourself. It is a fascinating riddle."

Reuben walked to Anam's side of the table. He carefully studied the words inscribed upon the lambskin, then took two steps backwards. "I think you'd better leave," he demanded, his voice trembling with emotion.

"What?" Anam was confused. "But I haven't finished eating ... and I still have to pay you. How much do I owe?"

His eyes cold, Reuben said, "Nothing. I want nothing from you. Just leave this place at once. Please."

Anam was shocked by the man's sudden change of heart. "Have I offended you in some way?" he asked.

The young man refused to answer. Anam left some coins on the table to pay for his meal, and then went on his way, perplexed by this abrupt turn of events.

For the rest of the day, as he walked about the little town seeking answers, the hostility of the townspeople seemed to follow him wherever he would go. At first, when he would simply state that he was seeking information about his family, they would respond in a friendly and helpful manner. But as soon as he would mention the inscription on the lambskin, they turned their backs and walked away, often cursing. One man even spat upon him. Anam's instinct was to punch the man in retaliation, but he restrained himself. A stranger in town—and one whom nobody seemed to like—he was obviously outnumbered and would surely end up on the losing side of any confrontation.

After a while he stopped mentioning the lambskin. Still, he made no progress. Nobody was forthcoming with any information that might help him find out about his parents and the circumstances of his birth. Dejected, Anam arrived at the inn at the center of town just as dusk settled over the little hamlet. Tired from being on his feet all day, Anam was, at this point, just looking forward to a hot meal and a good night's rest.

The innkeeper was a short, plump old man named Johanan. "Are you here for lodging, stranger?" he asked.

"Yes," Anam replied. "And a meal, too, if you would be so kind. I have enough money to pay for both." He held out some gold coins his father had given him.

Johanan's eyes held suspicion. Ignoring the glittering money, he asked, "What is your name?"

Returning the money to a pouch beneath his garment, Anam avoided direct eye contact. "I am called Anam."

"Anam?" The innkeeper wrinkled his nose. "What a strange name. Tell me, who is your father? And from whence do you come?"

These were the same questions he had been answering for the townspeople all day. And each time, his honest reply, along with his own request for information, was met with nothing but contempt. There was no reason to believe things would be any different with this elderly gentleman, but Anam was committed to remaining honest. "My father is Micah, he is a prosperous merchant, and our home is many miles to the south of here."

Johanan scratched his balding head as his eyes carefully scrutinized Anam's face. "There is something familiar about you," he said thoughtfully. "I feel as if I have seen you before. Tell me, have you accompanied your father here on business perhaps?"

"Yes, sir," he replied. "But we never spent any time here in Bethlehem. We only passed through town."

"Yet, somehow, your face reminds me of a man I once knew."

Now Anam's curiosity was running rampant. It could not be Micah he resembled, for he was not his "real" father, at least not in the biological sense. Was the innkeeper remembering the man from whose seed he was conceived? Anam decided this was a good opportunity to speak frankly regarding the purpose of his visit. "Sir, may we sit down?"

The old man smiled. "Of course. In fact, you came just in time for the evening meal. My wife is ill and will not be joining me at my table tonight." His smile vanished when he spoke of his sick wife. Then regaining his composure he said, "Come, let us sit and eat together."

Two servants brought them food in the dimly lit dining room. There was roasted lamb along with fresh bread and goat cheese. After bowing their heads in prayer, they began eating. The innkeeper took a sip of his wine. "Now, where were we? Oh yes, you were going to tell me why you are here."

Anam swallowed a piece of meat. It tasted wonderful. He cleared his throat and began. "I think I may know why I look familiar to you."

Johanan sipped his wine without taking his eyes off the younger man across the table from him.

"My father Micah is a good and kind man. However, he and I do not share the same lineage. My real parents, I believe, are from here in Bethlehem." Anam then went on to explain the story that Micah had told to him—how as a baby he had been found on the roadside along with the dead woman who most likely was his mother. He also showed him the lambskin with the inscription. This man seemed friendlier than the others, so perhaps his reaction would be different. But as soon as Johanan read the inscription, his face paled as if he had seen a ghost, and he averted his eyes.

Anam quickly put the lambskin away and tried to salvage their conversation, though he feared he would now, once again, be rebuffed. "So," he concluded, "perhaps the reason I look familiar to you is because you once knew the man who is my father by blood. Please, sir, I beseech you, do you recall his name?"

"I'm afraid my memory is not as sharp as it was in my younger years," said Johanan. "Maybe my mind is just playing tricks on me."

Anam noticed a drastic change in the old man's demeanor after he'd related his story—especially after he had shown him the lambskin. It was as if now he wanted nothing to do with this newcomer. But Anam was determined not to give up so easily. He had come too far. Looking Johanan straight in the eyes, he pleaded, "Please tell me more. As an elder of this town I am sure you know the circumstances of what happened here about thirty years ago, shortly after I was born."

Johanan finished his wine and ordered a servant to bring more. The pleasant mood between the two men had turned stone cold, and silence reigned between them until Johanan's second glass of wine arrived. He drank some, put down the glass, and said, "Listen. I should not be sharing such evil with you. But against my better judgment, I will."

"Evil?" Anam was dumfounded.

"Yes, evil. That inscription brings back terrible memories of an awful time. A great period of violence and suffering that tore at the very heart of our peaceful little village."

Anam swallowed hard.

Johanan stared across the room, immersed in his memories, relating the tale as if he were reliving it before his own eyes. "The one of whom the inscription speaks … all the killing was because of him."

"Do you mean …" Anam's voice cracked and his throat became dry, "Jesus?"

The old man glared at him. "Do not utter that name in my presence," he thundered, "or I will have my servants throw you out into the night!"

"Sir, I'm sorry. I meant no offense."

There was an awkward, strained silence for a dozen heartbeats. The servants out in the kitchen bustled about noisily, as if pretending they could not hear what was being said.

"Well … anyway," grumbled the innkeeper as he finished his second glass of wine and ordered a third. "The last time I heard anyone use that name was many years ago. It was those foolish shepherds with their tall tales that led to the soldiers coming here, and with them such wanton bloodshed and death."

"Please tell me more. Who were these shepherds? What did they do to provoke the soldiers? Were they criminals?"

Johanan shook his head. "Not in the strict sense of the word, I suppose. But what they provoked was worse than anything I've ever seen by any mere criminal. Even a thief at least has a purpose for the bad deeds he does. These fools, on the other hand, had no reason for spreading their vile delusions. No reason, that is, other than the corruption of their own drunken minds."

This last comment, thought Anam, sounded a bit ironic as the old man was now well into his third glass of wine. But he implored Johanan to continue; he was spellbound by what he was hearing.

"In fact, it was right around this time of the year, as I recall. These shepherds, about twelve of them, came into town with a fantastic story. All made the same claim. They said they were visited by an angel."

Anam's eyes widened. "An angel?"

Johanan finished his glass of wine. "Ha! Is that not the height of foolishness? Why would an angel of the Most High visit such lowly men? Tell me, would you not think, if he were to send a messenger, would it not be to the important men? Those with power?"

With a shrug, Anam said, "My father has always told me that the Lord works in mysterious ways. Maybe he had a special reason for the angelic visit."

The innkeeper shook his head. "Wait. You will not want to defend these wicked men and make excuses for them after you hear the rest of the story. They stormed into town telling everyone that a heavenly host had come to announce the birth of the Messiah—right here in Bethlehem!"

The food on Anam's plate remained almost untouched. He was fascinated by the old man's tale and could no longer focus on eating. What could all of this have to do with the circumstances of his own birth, and what befell his parents?

Johanan continued, "I didn't believe them, of course. But many of the townspeople did. Soon word spread throughout Judea, and even to more distant lands. People came from miles around to see the poor child whom the shepherds claimed to be the Messiah.

"Although I didn't believe the shepherds, I kept my mouth shut. A clever innkeeper knows a good thing. Many of the visitors required a place to stay. They needed to eat. My inn overflowed with paying customers. It lasted for months! My purse spilled over with the money I earned. Even the census couldn't compare to those days.

"The last to come were three powerful and mysterious men from far-off countries. The caravan was so long … I stood on the roof and still couldn't see the end of the procession. Never had Bethlehem been showered with so much honor.

"And then …" Johanan's voice grew bitter. "Well … let's just say that nobody believes the shepherds' story any longer, especially after what happened next."

"Is what happened next the reason you say these men were doers of evil, and not just harmless drunkards?"

Johanan nodded his head vigorously. "Yes indeed, that is correct. By saying that the Messiah had come, the shepherds provoked the wrath of Herod, who became jealous. The king determined to stop what he saw as a threat to his own power and resolved to kill this newborn future king. He ordered his soldiers to murder every male infant in Bethlehem, also in the surrounding countryside. They came, and …" The old man's eyes filled with tears. He tried to continue, but was too choked up with emotion.

Anam felt awful for dredging up such terrible memories for this man. Yet he had one more question that he needed answered, and even though he wanted to cause no further hurt to the innkeeper, he asked nonetheless. "My good sir, I beg you, please tell me, does the inscription I showed you somehow bear witness to these horrific events?"

Johanan's eyes shifted from sadness to anger. "Without a doubt," he said. "The name on that lambskin of yours ... you know the one."

Tentatively, in a quiet voice Anam muttered, "Jesus?" knowing how much the man across the table from him hated that name.

An angry nod confirmed it.

"The shepherds said that this ... Jesus, was the promised Messiah?"

"Yes! And that is why all the killing happened," said Johanan, rubbing his eyes. "Now, I have told you enough. You may have a room for the night if you wish. But no more of this talk about bad things. It is all in the past and we cannot change what has happened."

Anam still had many questions. Now, more than ever, he had to find out all he could about this child Jesus, and why his birth had caused such a tumult. Then a thought came to him. The shepherds! He would confront them and find out the truth. He asked the innkeeper where he might find them.

Johanan sighed deeply. "In fact, I happen to know that they return to this area, to the outskirts of town, this time every year. But my friend, as I have told you, they are bad men. If you are a righteous man, you will want nothing to do with them."

"I do not fear them," he boldly declared. Actually, that was not entirely true. He was more than a little worried to face these rough herdsmen who were responsible for so much killing, not to mention the fact that they were responsible for his own unfortunate circumstances. Yet something deep inside compelled him forward.

Reluctantly, the innkeeper gave directions to where Anam would find the shepherds camped out at their winter feeding grounds.

Anam thanked the old man and retired to his room for the night. In silent prayer he implored God for his guidance and protection. Tomorrow promised to bring him the answers he had asked himself his entire life. He felt as if he had just made a date with his own destiny.

4

CHAPTER

$\mathscr{A}$nam awoke with the sun, feeling as if he hadn't slept at all. He had spent the night wrestling with his coverings. Sleep came in fits and starts as he kept wondering what it would be like when he found the shepherds. Would his courage fail him at the critical moment? Would he turn and run rather than confront them with the questions he was burning to ask?

As he dressed, visions of what his mother's last days must have been like haunted him. She had sacrificed her own life in order to save his. What bravery … and how unnecessary. These foolish men and their tall tales were the cause of all the death and suffering. What would he say to them? If they knew he was there to accuse them of complicity in his mother's death, they would be unlikely to surrender much information. He tried to think of a plan, but nothing came to him. Finally, he paid the innkeeper and set off on his journey.

The winter feeding grounds, according to the innkeeper's directions, were only a mile or two outside of Bethlehem. As soon as he made his way behind the inn and past the foul-smelling caves that were used as stables to shelter animals in the winter, the road veered off and led into a vacant, hilly land where not another soul could be seen. The sun was climbing in the eastern sky, yet a chill clung to the air, especially when the early-morning breeze kicked up. With each passing step Anam knew he was drawing closer to the shepherds' encampment, and he felt his heart rate ramping up. The fear of the unknown gripped him and would not let go. Still, he trudged forward, expecting to see something around each curve and over each hill. But all there was for the eye to see were barren pastures and still more hills.

The road became a rough trail, with no markings to distinguish it. He had to step carefully to avoid twisting his ankle on the many rocks and stones.

After an hour of walking, he grew a bit hungry. He had been so eager to get going that morning, he had skipped breakfast. Anam sat on a large boulder, placing his sack of belongings next to him. He breathed in the cool, clear air and held it in his lungs for a moment. It felt good as he slowly exhaled. He was thinking of eating some of the loaves he had brought with him when he thought he heard something. Cupping his ear with his hand, he strained to hear more clearly. Sheep! Unmistakably, that is what he heard. There were sheep bleating in the distance.

Well, he thought, there would be no turning back now. The winter pasture must be close by, probably right over the next hill. Forgetting all about his hunger, Anam gathered up his provisions and set off at a run toward the hill. He stopped, out of breath, as he nearly crested it. He was not ready to make his appearance just yet. First he needed to gain control of his breathing and slow down his racing heart. Letting the shepherds see him like this would betray a sign of weakness, which was the last thing he wanted to do.

He found a scrubby little patch of bushes. Sitting on the ground beneath their meager shade, he closed his eyes and sought God. *I have come this far*, he said to his unseen Creator. *Please do not let me fail now. Please, Lord, after so many years, let me find the courage to learn the truth. I want to move on with my life, but that cannot happen if I do not go through with this. I beg of you, God, make your strength my strength, and I will not fear these harsh men, nor turn away from them. Thank you, Lord. Amen.*

Without further hesitation, Anam rose and made his way the remaining distance to the top of the hill. The wind blew his hair as he scanned the vast area before him. Off to his right he saw the sheep grazing calmly in the late-morning sun. But where were the shepherds? He walked down the back side of the hill, his eyes scouring the land for any sign of them.

At the bottom of the hill he thought he smelled smoke, and his heart quickened because he knew they were not far away. He crept through some bushes and saw five men clustered in a semi-circle around a campfire. They spotted him at the same moment he saw them. "Looks like we have a visitor," said one of the younger shepherds.

Anam stepped out of the bushes, determined not to let them see how nervous he was.

"Come and share some breakfast with us, friend," said one of the older ones, a thin man with a thick gray beard.

Anam approached cautiously. "My name is Anam." He waited, expecting them to greet his name with the same unfriendly curiosity he'd grown accustomed to. Surprisingly, they didn't. In fact, it didn't seem to mean anything to them. They just smiled.

He walked over to the little group and sat down with them.

"My name is Eli," said the oldest of them, whom Anam surmised was their leader. Another man handed him a cup of sheep's milk and some cheese, which he gladly accepted. Eli then introduced the other shepherds. "There are still others amongst our group," he said, "but they have not yet arrived."

Anam remembered what the innkeeper had told him about the shepherds returning to this same place every year. He decided to jump right in with a question and to forego the small talk. "Oh, so you mean all of you come from afar? You do not live here?"

He sipped his milk, examining the small band of men over the rim of his cup. Some of them, especially the younger ones, seemed a bit fidgety and nervous, as if they did not like being asked questions such as this. It clearly made them uncomfortable.

The young shepherd who had first spotted him spoke up. His name was Jonas. "Perhaps we should be the ones to question you," he said, his voice edgier than before. "Who are you, and why have you come to our camp?"

Anam had been prepared to ask questions, not answer them. Then again, he was guilty of nothing, so why should he be afraid to reply? "I live many miles from here. But I have reason to believe that I may have been born in this area."

More than a few eyebrows were raised. One of the shepherds, a large man with big hands, asked in a calm voice, "Does your family hail from Bethlehem?"

Anam replied, "I cannot say for sure. In fact, that is why I am here. I have been told that you men might know about my family."

Jonas was still looking at him suspiciously, but the short, nearly bald man named Samuel said, "We are humble shepherds, Anam. But we will help if we can."

Before Anam could speak, Jonas piped up again. "Who told you we could help? The people of that town have never shown anything but hatred toward us. Why should we help you?"

Anam fixed his eyes upon the young man. *If they are all like him*, he thought, *it's easy to see how the townspeople dislike them so.*

"Please excuse our young friend," said Eli, putting down his bowl and looking at Anam with compassion. "He had an unfortunate encounter with some of the people of Bethlehem when he arrived here a few days ago. I am afraid it has put him in the wrong frame of mind. I assure you he means no offense."

"None taken," said Anam, realizing he may have been too hasty in judgment. He looked over at Jonas, who seemed to soften a bit.

"Actually," said Eli, "you have come here at the right time. A group of us meet in this place at this time each year for a special purpose. I am sure someone amongst our number will be able to help you." Eli let out a deep sigh as he stared thoughtfully into the fire. "When I was younger, we shepherds knew everyone in Bethlehem, and we were well regarded." He looked at Anam again. "That was long ago. But still, it's possible one of us may have known your relatives."

Anam finished his milk and put the cup down. Without being asked, Samuel rushed over and refilled it from his flask. "Thank you," Anam said quietly. He wanted to delve right into asking about his family. But it occurred to him that it would probably be best to befriend them first, before getting into any topics that might cause strife. "So, why do you gather here at this particular time of the year? Does it have something to do with caring for the sheep?"

They smiled at one another, as if sharing information they alone were privileged to know. "It is easier to show than to explain," answered Eli. "Tonight, when our brethren from neighboring territories join us, you are welcome to come as our guest." He smiled at Anam. "Then you will learn everything."

Anam spent the rest of the day in solitude, though the shepherds said he was welcome to make himself at home at their camp while they waited for their friends to arrive. Instead, he wandered the meadows in the surrounding countryside, lost in his own thoughts. The sun was shining pleasantly by the latter part of the afternoon, so Anam sat on a log to rest. He took some small cheeses Samuel had given him out of his sack and ate one of them. It was quite good. He laughed to himself. *At least I won't starve while I am out here with these fellows.* He was impressed by their hospitality. Did the people in town realize how gentle and harmless these men really were?

An eagle soared overhead in the nearly cloudless sky. The proud creature brought glory to God by its power and grace. Yes, even the animals had their own special place in creation. Unlike him. In moments of quiet like this, Anam felt more alone and out of place than usual. While his brothers were enjoying their lives and siring offspring to make their father Micah proud, here he was off in the middle of nowhere trying to learn about his own birth. Sometimes he even felt cursed. But whenever such a thought gripped him, he quickly dismissed it. To think that way would be to dishonor God, and that was something he would never do. "I will find out your plan for me, Lord," he murmured into the wind, "in your good time."

As the sun sank low in the west, Anam knew that soon he would meet with the shepherds again. This time there would be more of them, as they would be joined by the rest of their group.

He got up and began walking. For a while, his thoughts were happy. Things were turning out better than he could have hoped. These men were so cooperative, and maybe they would indeed be able to help him. But then doubts subtly crept into his consciousness. He really didn't know these men well, having only met them a few hours earlier. Maybe they were the good ones, and the evildoers were those assembling just over that hill up ahead at this very moment. His father had warned him that bad men always committed their unrighteous deeds at night, under the cloak of darkness. "They hate the light," the old man had warned him, "because the light reveals their sin."

Fear crept over him like an ill wind. *Maybe I should turn and leave*, he thought as he approached the top of the hill above their encampment. With the rapidly gathering darkness he began to struggle with his worries even more. *There are no civilized people for miles around. I could be killed out here and nobody would know it. If I do not return, will Father come looking for me? What about my brothers? Do they really think of me as family enough to care about my fate? What if …*

"There you are!" A cheerful voice snapped him out of his thoughts.

Jonas stood directly in front of him. "Eli was worried about you," he said, reaching out to grasp Anam's shoulder. "He sent me out to look for you. And to ask your forgiveness for my behavior this morning."

Relief swept over Anam as he realized the young man's sincerity. "As I told you, I took no offense. I'm certain you have good reason to be wary of strangers."

As they walked together over the top of the hill and down the other side toward the clearing, they engaged in friendly conversation. "I have never been a hateful man," said Jonas. "But it is hard not to feel bitter when others mean you harm simply for who you are."

Anam contemplated his words as they walked along in the cool air, the last rays of the sun swiftly disappearing behind the hills. "I have heard about the hatred these people in Bethlehem have toward you, and I think I know the reason for it." As soon as the words had left his mouth, he wished he hadn't uttered them. The last thing he wanted was to insult this youth now that he had befriended him.

But Jonas merely shook his head. "It is because they do not know the full story. They do not know the truth."

Anam didn't push the subject. They had arrived at the shepherds' campsite, which was now a loud gathering of more than a dozen men.

Eli and Samuel greeted Anam warmly and introduced him to the newly arrived shepherds. After sharing a communal meal, at which Eli delivered one of the most beautiful prayers of thanks Anam had ever heard, they all sat around a roaring campfire. Its heat felt good, and its light commingled with that of the full moon to turn the night into a pale reflection of the day.

One by one the more elderly of the shepherds began to speak. The reason for their gathering became immediately clear, and it was intricately linked to the story Anam wanted to hear—their tale of being visited by an angel and all that followed. It had happened at this very same time of year, thirty years ago now. Ever since, they had all gathered together at this place each year during this same week to recall and celebrate what all of them ardently considered blessed events. One by one, they recounted their experiences.

The last to speak was Eli, who, though a simple man, spoke in words of profound eloquence. He began, "I will recall that holy night for as long as I live …"

5

CHAPTER

$\mathscr{A}$nam had spent many memorable evenings around a campfire. In his travels with Micah and his brothers, he loved the warm glow of the fire, and the glow he felt inside as he and his brothers would tell stories, poke fun at each other, laugh, and sometimes sing, well into the night. But this campfire gathering was like nothing Anam had ever experienced. He was not prepared for the deep feeling and reverence these men demonstrated as they shared their memories of a night so long ago. They were clearly not the type to show their emotions easily. They were coarse men accustomed to life in the wilderness with very few comforts, men who would not hesitate to defend the sheep from lions, bears, or armed thieves at the risk of their own safety. Yet tonight they were more like youngsters listening with delight to a beloved children's tale.

As Eli began his account, a hushed silence enveloped the group. Only Eli's voice and the crackling fire could be heard.

I was much younger back then, of course, and I required very little sleep, so I was happy to accept the duty of keeping watch at night. The air was cold and clear, just as it is this evening. I pulled my cloak up around me and strolled about the meadow. The sheep under my charge lay fast asleep. As I watched the gentle creatures in their peaceful slumber, I wondered, "Do animals have dreams the way men do?" I laughed, thinking that all a sheep would probably dream about would be greener pastures. But I, as a young man, indeed had dreams—many of them. I envisioned myself traveling to far-off lands, doing exciting things and going on one adventure after another. Yet I knew nothing remarkable was likely to happen in my life. As a shepherd, like my father before me and his father before him, my life would always be a simple existence, tending to the sheep day in and day out and not much more.

I was pondering these things while staring at the clear night sky. There were so many stars out that night, more than a man could ever count. To pass the time I began connecting the stars to one another with imaginary lines in my mind. Some became great sailing ships, others lions or bears. If I really stretched my imagination I could even see mighty fortresses and glorious palaces. A few of these shiny points of light came together to form sheep. Ah yes, always back to the sheep …

Anam noticed the men around the fire all smiled and nodded in agreement. One of them tossed a large piece of wood on the fire. The orange flames radiated a warm glow that felt good to Anam, since the air had turned cold with the darkness. Eli continued …

But then something happened, a brightening of the sky that startled me. At first it seemed my eyes were playing tricks on me. I had most likely gone far too long without sleep, and my weary mind was not serving me well. Yet what I was seeing was no illusion. This was really happening! A powerful beam of light was descending from the heavens, bathing with its splendor a spot behind a tree about a hundred feet away, making it whiter than the snows of Mount Hermon.

I stood there, frozen as stiff as a statue. My jaw hung open, my eyes wide with wonder. I did not understand what was happening, but something deep inside told me that I was in the midst of a presence beyond the natural, not of this earth.

The light grew even more intense, flooding out the rays of the moon and the twinkling of the stars. My instincts suddenly took over, and I dropped my staff and dashed off to summon the others. Running as fast as I could, within moments I was back at the little shelter where we slept. Out of breath, I called the others out to see what was happening. Those who were still awake ran out immediately, while the others rose groggily from their slumber.

"What are you rambling about?" one of the elders grumbled. "Listen, if this is your idea of a joke, I'm telling you right now that ..."

Before he could finish, another man interrupted, pointing toward the light, "Look!"

The rest of the men turned in stunned amazement. The light now encompassed the entire area near the tree. Some of the men cowered in fear; others shielded their eyes with their hands and stared at the incredible sight.

"Come, follow me," I said, then ran off, the others right behind me. There were twelve of us. We stopped directly in front of the tree, which was now lit up brighter than noontime, yet with a brilliance unlike the sun. It was the middle of the night, but we had to shield our eyes from the brightness. This was a heavenly light—that is the only way I can describe it.

Someone declared, "I see a form like a body!"

"It is an angel!" I shouted, and I fell to my knees. All around me my brethren likewise dropped to the ground, the older men pushing their faces hard against the grass in fear. In fact, we were all afraid and trembling.

Anam turned his attention to the other shepherds around the fire as the flames cast a flickering glow across their faces. Only a few of the men there had been with Eli that fateful night, and it was easy to tell who they were. Tears had begun to well up in their eyes, and some already had streams flowing down their cheeks. They seemed to be reliving the events of thirty years past as Eli went on with his story …

We all knew in our hearts that we were in the presence of a heavenly messenger. But why had he come here? To us, of all people! We were but lowly shepherds. Was there sin in our lives? Had the Lord sent his angel to rebuke us? All of us were praying silently, hoping for mercy as we waited for whatever might happen next. I remember holding my breath for what seemed a very long time.

Then we heard a voice. To my ears, it seemed to convey sweetness and authority in the same instant. It was the voice of a young man, but somehow unlike any I had ever heard. "Be not afraid," it said. "I bring to you tidings of great joy."

Up until that point, my eyes had been cast toward the ground. I was afraid to gaze upon this powerful angel of the Lord.

But the tone and quality of his voice was soothing, and it removed all of my fear. Still on my knees, I lifted my eyes up toward him and beheld the splendor of his beauty.

This angelic being had the form and the countenance of a man, but in a way far beyond the glory of an average man. His wings were like those of a large white dove, only much brighter, and they were fluttering with a rhythmic grace that would be impossible to describe. He had the face of one whose dwelling place was in the heavens, far beyond the abode of mortal man. The expression upon that face reinforced his words. He was not here to condemn us. Quite to the contrary, he had appeared to us on that night to make a joyful announcement that would change our lives, and indeed the entire world.

The others were as engrossed as I was, hanging on to his every word. It was clear to us now that this was a momentous and most blessed event.

In a kind yet powerful voice, the angel proclaimed, "Today, in the City of David, the Savior has been born."

We were awestruck by his words. The Savior! I couldn't believe my ears. All of Israel had awaited this day for many ages, long before even our fathers' fathers were born.

As he spoke, the angel seemed to become even brighter, which I would not have thought possible. I could hear the joy in his voice, and I understood that he took great pleasure in delivering this magnificent news to us. I then heard him say, "The Savior who is Christ—Christ the Lord."

At the mention of that name, the angel's voice became rich with adoration. He crossed his wings and bowed his head in a sign of utmost reverence. Then he spoke to us again. "This shall be a sign unto you," he said with a smile that could melt the hardest of hearts. "You will recognize Him thus: In a poor stable behind Bethlehem you will find a baby in swaddling clothes, in a manger for animals, as there was no room for the Messiah in the City of David."

I was trying to comprehend all that I was hearing. No room for the Messiah? What an outrage! At that moment I wanted nothing more than to find Him and honor Him in any way that I could. But before I could think any further, the angel was joined by what must have been the entire host of heaven. All of them bright, powerful, and beautiful heavenly beings, they descended upon the earth like a great whirlwind. The air was filled with the other-worldly splendor of their ethereal singing. They were singing the songs of heaven as they illuminated the night skies above with their glorious presence. These were songs of praise sung by lips that had known not sin. Truly, I thought, how pleasing such a magnificent chorus must sound to the ears of Almighty God. As the singing grew louder, I recognized the words, "Glory to God in the highest heaven, and peace on earth to men of good will."

Subtly at first, and then more swiftly, the great light before us began to diffuse. With it, the sound of singing receded until it faded away completely and we were once again alone.

Anam realized that the others were listening as intently as he was to Eli's story. It was clear that they all considered this a most blessed event. Some of them were weeping uncontrollably. These were big, brawny, rough herdsmen—weeping! And yet the people of Bethlehem claim that they are lying about the angelic visit. If it were a lie, why would they get so emotional when remembering that night? For the first time Anam began to wonder if their story was true. And if so, what did it all mean? He leaned in closer as Eli continued his story …

After the angels ascended back to heaven, I slowly made my way back onto my feet, as did the others. Within minutes we were all murmuring to one another, trying to decide what we should do, still shocked by what we had just beheld. "We must go and find this stable at once," I declared. The others agreed, intent to obey God's word.

Simon then told us about an encounter he'd had earlier in the day. He'd seen a woman, heavy with child, soon to give birth. She and her husband were looking for lodging in town, but were unable to find any. So Simon told them about the stable.

We all agreed that this must be the child the angel had told us about. We gathered up whatever provisions we could offer to this little family—some bread, milk, cheese, and a lambskin blanket—and set off in great haste toward the stable. We left the flock behind, knowing the task before us was far more important.

We quickly made our way over the hills with the light of a great star, much brighter than any I had ever seen, to guide our way. Bypassing the sleeping town, we approached the stable behind the inn. When we arrived, none of us seemed to have the courage to go inside. The others began to prod me saying, "Eli, you were the first to see the angel. You go in."

I took a step forward, and then stopped dead in my tracks. "But, but I do not know what to say."

"Just tell them that an angel sent us here," said Benjamin, the eldest of our group, "and that we have come to bring gifts, and to worship the Messiah."

Still I hesitated. I knew what we were doing was good, but never in my life had I been in the presence of greatness, and I was too afraid.

"At least take a look," Benjamin whispered. "If you are very quiet they will not even know you are there."

The others all nodded in silent agreement. I gathered up my courage and crept toward a tiny opening from where I could see the inside of the stable. Benjamin was right behind me.

"Well," he asked impatiently, "what do you see?"

"I see a young woman. Ah, she is as beautiful as the angels. Her baby is nearby, crying. She is speaking to him in a way that almost sounds like singing." I didn't know exactly how to describe it to the others, but it was a voice unlike any I had ever heard. It was clear to me that the bond between mother and child was even stronger than that which is ordained by nature. Her words were comforting to the tiny babe, and as she picked him up and held him in her arms, he cooed in contentment.

Benjamin nudged me. "Go inside and introduce yourself," he whispered in my ear. "Then we will come in and join you."

But before I had a chance to move, a tall man appeared in the entrance. He wore the humble garment of an ordinary man, yet something about him was of a regal bearing. The man eyed me with suspicion, then looked at the others standing behind me. "Who is there?" he demanded, blocking the entrance protectively.

My voice caught in my throat a moment before I managed to say, "Sir, we are shepherds. We have come to bring food for you and a lambskin blanket for the child." Then I added, as reverently as I could, "And most importantly, to adore the Savior."

A smile of recognition crossed the man's handsome face. "I am Joseph," he said, and he stepped aside to let us in.

The others followed timidly, and we made our way to the young mother and child. The infant was falling asleep in her arms as she sat on some loose hay on the cold, damp ground. "I am Mary," she said softly. "We are pleased to have visitors."

One of the younger boys walked up to her and placed some of the food at her feet. She smiled warmly at the youth. "God will remember your kindness, young man." Then she looked at the rest of us with that same sweet smile. "And yours—each of you."

I then remembered the blanket we had brought with us. I removed it from the sack we carried it in and laid it at her feet. "Mother, please take this lambskin blanket. It will keep your precious son warm. I prepared it for my own child who is about to be born, but I want you to have it … for the Savior."

She reached out and patted my hand warmly. Her skin was smooth and soft. "We have no way to repay you for your generosity," she said as she wrapped the baby in the blanket.

Joseph was standing nearby. "That is true," he said. "All we can offer is our sincere gratitude."

Then Benjamin said, "There is one thing that you can do for us."

Joseph looked at him curiously.

"Please allow us to worship the Messiah." Benjamin's old eyes filled with tears.

Gently rocking the tiny baby in her arms, Mary looked at us and asked, "How is it that you men have knowledge of this?"

Benjamin began to speak, but he was too overcome with emotion. I spoke up, and told her the story of the angels and the message they had delivered unto us.

Upon hearing my words, she smiled knowingly at Joseph, and he returned the gaze. "You men are the first of many to hear the truth," he said. "What the prophets of old foretold has come to pass this night."

Mary looked upon all of us, one at a time, with eyes full of love and compassion. "Tell me your names, each of you. I will remember your kindness, and tell Jesus about you when he is older."

One by one, we humbly stepped forward and she allowed us to kiss the hem of his garment. We each told her our name as we did so. Before we finally left, she said to us, "The Lord will be with you all of your lives. Come hardship, oppression, or any difficulty, rest assured that he will always be with you."

Joseph nodded his agreement, smiled at us, and said, "Go in peace."

We all promised to come again, and to tell others what we were told by the angel, so that many more would come to worship Jesus. And with that we set off once again back toward the sheepfold.

Anam was captivated by Eli's account of the wondrous event. But the feeling didn't last long. He noticed Eli's expression suddenly changed from that of ecstatic joy to deep anxiety. It was as if a painful memory had suddenly flooded Eli's mind and had completely replaced the joyful thoughts of just a moment before. As the other men around the campfire jubilantly talked amongst themselves, Anam watched as Eli looked into the glowing embers of the dying fire and let out a deep sigh. Then Eli said something to himself that Anam could barely make out: "I wish I knew that he still lives."

6
CHAPTER

This had been the most amazing evening of Anam's life. What he found most remarkable were the words attributed to the angel. They were very similar to the words written upon the lambskin that was the only clue to his birth. "Glory to God in the highest heaven, and peace on earth to men of good will, through Jesus Christ, who was born of Mary in a stable in Bethlehem and who, wrapped in swaddling clothes, was in a manger, he who is the Savior of the world."

This Jesus seemed to be at the heart of so much controversy. The shepherds adored him and claimed he was the promised Messiah. Yet the people of Bethlehem reviled him and refused to even speak his name. Anam was confused. What was the truth? Why was this mysterious Jesus so important? And how did this all fit into his own life?

Anam was, however, now very sure of one thing. These shepherds were not evil. He heard the sincerity in their voices as each man gave his testimony about that night three decades earlier. These were not the drunken recollections of a vagabond group of reprobates. No; to the contrary, the shepherds had demonstrated to Anam that they were quite genuine about what they believed. Of course, Anam supposed it was possible that somehow they were mistaken. Maybe there was some logical explanation for what they had seen. Yet whatever had transpired that night, Anam harbored no doubt that these men were honest, gentle souls who truly believed every word they had uttered.

They finished their gathering with fervent prayers and songs of praise to God, then retired to their tents for the evening. Eli offered Anam a place in his own tent, which he gratefully accepted. He had so many questions he wanted to ask Eli, but felt unsure of himself, not knowing exactly how he should phrase things. His reluctance reminded him of Moses, who said he was not a good speaker, but God allowed his brother Aaron to compensate for that deficiency. *But I have no real brothers to speak for me … and surely I am no Moses to begin with!*

As Anam wrestled with what to say, he heard the soft snoring of his tent-mate. He looked over and saw the old man fast asleep, his mouth slightly open. The slow and steady sound reminded him of his father. Anam had only left home a few days earlier, yet he missed Micah already. Though not his father by blood, this man who found him as a baby had shown him genuine paternal love his entire life. Was it a betrayal, seeking to find his "true" father? It hurt to think he might be offending the only father he had ever known. Yet Micah had given Anam his blessing to go on this journey, so he knew the guilt he was feeling was unjustified.

Why, then, he asked himself, did he feel such tension at this moment? Perhaps the idea of at last finding out the truth about his origins frightened him. After all, his entire life he had carried this great mystery within himself. In a way, it had become a part of him. Now that was about to change. Would it mean he was no longer part of Micah's family? Would this new revelation change his life in ways he did not want? His heart was filled with the joy of anticipation along with the dread of the unknown.

He tried to rest, but sleep escaped him. Finally, he rose and quietly slipped out of the tent. The night was cold, and ablaze with starlight. Anam walked to the far edge of the encampment, past the dozing sheep, and found a small cluster of trees. He wondered if this was the spot where the shepherds had seen the angel. No longer did he think in terms of them "claiming" they saw an angel; he honestly believed their words were true. He could discern nothing deceitful about these men.

Anam cast his eyes on the great constellations of stars shining down from the vault of heaven. There was no angel in the fields tonight. None that he could see, at least. His father had often told him that multitudes of God's angels roamed the earth at all times, offering their protection and guidance to all the righteous. Anam frequently imagined that guardian angels followed his every movement, keeping him safe from enemies and helping him avoid pitfalls. The thought had always brought him great comfort and peace of mind.

But the angel described by Eli and the other shepherds was of a visible form, or at least he revealed himself in such a way. He looked like a man, though glorified far beyond that of mere flesh and blood. If only such a being would come to him now, surely one so powerful could answer all his questions. He looked up into the heavens, almost as if expecting a vision. Alas, the skies remained in a natural state. No singing choirs of the heavenly host, no celestial lights. Just a cold winter's night, and one man standing alone with his unanswered questions.

To keep warm, he ambled about the rolling meadows and rubbed his hands together. His tired mind wandered back to the one period in his life when he thought that, just maybe, he could find true happiness and contentment.

In assisting his father with his merchant business, they had on numerous occasions traveled to a great trading center many miles away on the shores of the sea. There Micah engaged in commerce with a wealthy man named Isaac, with whom he traded all kinds of valuable goods from ports near and far. Both men prospered much from these lucrative transactions.

On one of these trips, when Anam was about nineteen, he met a young woman whom he later discovered was Isaac's daughter. She had a keen sense of math, and though it was not at all the norm for women to do such work, this remarkable girl helped her father keep accurate accounts for his business. Anam learned that her name was Judith, and he was smitten when he first laid eyes on her. Such a smooth complexion she had, and thick, dark hair, finer than any he had ever seen. Beyond her physical beauty, she had a wit and intelligence about her that he found intriguing.

The two struck up a friendship, and before long, the inevitable flame of young love ignited.

Wanting to do what was proper and fitting, and what his heart was calling him to do, Anam went to his father and told him that he would like permission to ask for this girl's hand in marriage.

Anam recalled the old man's reaction as if it were only yesterday. His expression somber, Micah slowly shook his head. "I am afraid that is not possible, my son."

Anam's countenance shrank into sadness. "But why? Is she yet betrothed to another?"

"No."

Befuddled and desperately disappointed, Anam asked, "Is it something I have done? Did I offend her or her family in any way?"

"No."

Both were silent, until Micah finally told him the truth. "Anam, there are certain things in life that do not seem fair. It is best that you come to know this at a young age. The girl's father would never permit you to marry his daughter. His bloodline is of a long and noble heritage. He will see to it that her husband is a man whose seed can continue that noble bloodline."

In his innocence, Anam had naively said, "But Father, our family is also of noble heritage. Can I not, therefore, be such a man?"

Micah put his hand on Anam's shoulder. "You know that ever since I first took you home, I have considered you my son. And so I shall, till my dying breath." He sighed heavily. "But the world does not see it that way. Your real father is unknown, so we cannot say who you are. Your children would have no heritage. Perhaps we can find a girl whose family is of no distinction. Then we ..."

Anam had obediently listened to the rest of what his father had to say, but the damage had been done. Even now, many years later, Micah's words echoed painfully through the corridors of his mind: *Your real father is unknown.*

As Anam shivered in the cold night air, he hugged himself for warmth and began to make his way back to the camp. He wondered if he would ever be able to shake off the feeling that he was not whole, that he was like a tree without roots. Such a tree, if it could exist at all, would not survive long. It would have no way to sustain itself. It would wither away and die, and no one would even remember it was ever there. Anam felt as if his soul were without roots, drifting aimlessly, awaiting a future of nothingness.

As he shuffled along, he came to Eli's tent. To his surprise, he saw a faint flickering of light inside. He poked his head through the folds of the tent and found the old man hunched over large scrolls of parchment, a small lamp his only source of light. His thoughts immediately turned to Micah, who also had a great devotion to the Word of God.

"I beg your pardon," Anam said, bowing his head as he stepped inside. "I did not mean to intrude."

Eli looked up at him. "No intrusion at all, my son. As you age, you will find that it is difficult to maintain sleep throughout the night." The old shepherd smiled. "Though it seems you yourself are not able to sleep either."

Anam took a step closer and Eli beckoned him to sit, which he did. In the darkness of the tent, the dancing flame from the lamp cast a faint light on the men's faces. "I could not rest—not after all I have heard this evening."

Eli's face beamed. "So, you enjoyed hearing of our miraculous encounter?"

Though he would not have phrased it that way, it was true. Anam was indeed intrigued by this story of the angel and the newborn King. But the evil that followed afterward remained a stumbling block and a source of great pain.

"I liked one part in particular. Where you recited the words that the angel from on high spoke to you."

Anam reached into his bag, carefully retrieved the lambskin blanket, and unfolded it with reverence. He held it before Eli's eyes. The old man read the words aloud. His face took on the look of stunned amazement as he did so. "Where did you find this?"

"My father ... well, the man I call my father ... found it wrapped around me when I was an infant. The woman we presume was my mother lay dead beside me. It appeared she gave her life trying to save mine. Do you think the words on this blanket connect me or my family to this Jesus somehow? I feel as if I have been drawn to you to find the answer."

Looking up, Eli closed his eyes and muttered a prayer of thanks. Returning his gaze to Anam, he said, "Indeed, you have been sent here for the answers you seek. It is all becoming very clear to me now. I knew your father. In fact, I knew him very well."

Anam's mind overflowed with exhilaration on hearing these last words. In all his life, this was the first person he had ever met with direct knowledge about one of his parents. He could feel his heart beat faster with anticipation. Eli did not make him wait a moment longer.

"Your father was my master. I used to care for his sheep."

"Please, tell me more," Anam said with excitement.

"How fortunate I am to be able to tell you, his son, what a wonderful man he was," said Eli, doing his best to fight back tears. "He loved you and your mother very much. The two of you were the light of his life. I vividly recall how he beamed with pride and joy over your birth, his first and only son. Ah, he was such a happy man."

Anam was fixated by every word.

"Following the custom of our people, he performed the rite of circumcision on you and gave you the name, Stephen."

The greatest secret of his life had at last been revealed. He finally knew his real name. But there was still so much more to learn. He listened with rapt attention.

"Your father's name was Issachar, and he was a priest. He was a very important man in Bethlehem, the leader of the synagogue. He led worship services and officiated at marriages, funerals, and all the religious festivals and holy days. Issachar was the man people came to when they needed advice, and they all respected him for his wisdom and his knowledge of the things of God."

His mind whirling with a thousand questions, Anam first asked the one he had wondered about the most often over the years. "The woman we believe was my mother seems to have died protecting me. But what happened to my father? Did he survive?"

Up until now, Eli had seemed quite pleased to recount the details of his father's life. But his smile turned downward as he cleared his throat and spoke. "The sad answer is no, he did not. The relatives of those who were killed in the massacre took his life in revenge."

With those words, the last vestige of hope Anam had that his father might yet be alive vanished into thin air. He soon felt his sadness quickly turn to anger. "But you said he was a leader in the town, well-respected for his wisdom. Why, then, would they kill him? I do not understand."

Eli sighed and nodded toward the scrolls laid out before him. "What happened to your father is the same thing that happened to these holy men of old," he said, gesturing to the parchment. "He died for proclaiming the words of God."

Confused, Anam said, "My father was a prophet?"

Eli considered the question for a moment. "Not in the strictest sense of the word, perhaps. But the principle, I believe, is the same. Just as many of God's holy prophets were killed by the very people to whom they were sent to speak the truth, so your father died for proclaiming to the people of Bethlehem what he knew to be true."

It was all becoming clear to Anam now. "This has to do with Jesus, doesn't it?"

With a nod, Eli confirmed it. "Yes," he said. "Let me explain. You see, I was close to your father for many years. I knew him well. He was a just man, and was kind to me. In fact, he was one of the few people I have met who did not seem to care about one's station in life. He treated all with the same respect and dignity. So following our miraculous encounter with the angel, and after visiting the newborn King and his family, the first man I went to see was your father. I wanted him to be the first to hear the joyous news."

"And since he considered you a friend, he believed you?"

With a wide smile, the old shepherd said, "Oh, no. That was not the kind of man your father was. He had no reason to disbelieve me, but when it came to the things of God, he went to God himself for confirmation."

"What do you mean he went to God himself?"

"Let me explain. First, he came with me to see the child. Soon he became friendly with Joseph and Mary, and came to realize that they were special people in God's plan. But even then he was not fully satisfied. You see, Anam, your father was very learned in the Torah. It was said that he could recite every word of it by memory, and I believe it. He scoured through the ancient prophecies for confirmation of the angel's words."

"Did he find them to be true?"

"Indeed he did," Eli said with a smile. "I remember as if it were yesterday, the morning he stood in front of the congregation at the synagogue and proclaimed that the day of redemption promised by God had come at last. He told the assembly that the holy words inspired by God in the sacred writings had confirmed that Jesus was the Messiah."

"And did they believe my father?" Anam felt his breathing quicken. It felt strange to be calling this man he had never met by the name of "father." Strange but wonderful.

"At first they did. They rejoiced in the good news he brought to them, and considered it to be a great honor that Bethlehem was the Savior's place of birth. But then ..." Eli stopped as his voice began to crack.

"Please, Eli. I must hear the rest of the story."

"And then came the great and terrible tragedy. Word of these events reached King Herod. And in his jealousy and zeal to protect his own power, he unleashed the wrath of his soldiers on the defenseless hamlet of Bethlehem."

"I ... I was told when I was in town how terrible and bloody the violence was. All those little babies murdered so senselessly ..."

The old man's eyes filled with pain. "That event came to be known as the Slaughter of the Innocents. Afterward, in their anger and grief, the townspeople went to your father and asked him if he still believed in this Jesus. They jeered at him and demanded that he renounce the name of this outsider who had brought nothing but death and destruction to their peaceful community."

Anam was silent for a moment. He was going to ask if his father then denied Jesus, but he felt he already knew the answer.

"Your father was a brave man, Anam. A bloodthirsty gang of grieving relatives gathered outside his synagogue and demanded that he curse the name of Jesus and repent of calling him the Messiah. But your father steadfastly refused, telling them that even death could not shake his convictions. The brutal mob picked up stones and assailed him without mercy. Then, in their murderous fury, the rabid crowd burned the synagogue to the ground with him inside. The ruins of this once splendid and holy building lie decaying on the ground to this day."

The sad story tore at Anam's heart. But there was still more he needed to know. "Eli, I believe my mother died the night of the slaughter. Was it as I have always thought … did she lose her life trying to save mine?"

"Yes. That is most likely what happened. Just before the massacre took place, your father left for Jerusalem, to tend to the synagogue's business in the Temple. Your mother,

Lydia, was a sweet and kind woman, and her love for you was beyond measure. I warned her that soldiers were coming, and she fled with you in the darkness, still in her nightclothes. The only possession she had with her was that blanket you now hold in your hands."

"You knew about this blanket? Please tell me its history, and how the words of the angel came to be written on it."

"That was the very lambskin we shepherds gave to Jesus on the night of his birth. Mary wrapped Baby Jesus in it on many cold nights. As you can imagine, that blanket meant a great deal to Mary. She and your mother had grown very close during the months before you were born. After your birth, Mary wanted to do something special for your mother, so she gave her that cherished blanket for you. It was truly a gift of love from her.

"Your father wrote those words on the lambskin in my presence. He wanted to write down what the angel had said, so I repeated the words to him. He was a clever and learned man, so he wrote the words in the form of a prayer, and as a testament to what he believed. He did this especially for you, so that you might come to believe when you were older."

Then Eli closed his eyes, turning his face up toward the heavens, and spoke the words on the lambskin from memory with great feeling. "Glory to God in the highest heaven, and peace on earth to men of good will, through Jesus Christ, who was born of Mary in a stable in Bethlehem and who, wrapped in swaddling clothes, was in a manger, he who is the Savior of the world." Tears streamed down Eli's face when he concluded the prayer.

Anam marveled to think that he and Jesus had shared the same blanket as newborn babes, and that his father believed this child was indeed the Messiah. It made Anam feel a special connection between himself and Jesus. He couldn't explain it, but he could feel it in the deepest part of his soul.

"Your father loved you very much," Eli said. "He said that if anything ever happened to him, I should tell you about Jesus when you were old enough to understand. But then you disappeared. We all assumed you were dead along with so many others."

Anam felt a shiver tremble through his body. All of this news was just too incredible to absorb at once.

The aging shepherd placed his hand on Anam's shoulder. "Yet now, in his perfect timing, the Lord has brought you here to me."

7
CHAPTER

$\mathscr{A}$nam spent a few days with the shepherds, learning all he could about his parents and his lineage. He desired to learn more about Jesus too, but the shepherds had not seen or heard from Jesus or his family since before Herod's slaughter. In fact, Eli couldn't even say for sure that Jesus was still alive. Yet the shepherds had gathered here to remember his birth. How strange that they would still cling to hope that Jesus was the promised Messiah so many years after he had disappeared.

Anam decided it was time for him to leave. He had discovered what he came here to learn. He not only knew his real name, he also knew the identity of his father and mother, and how and why they died. Yet this knowledge did not put his restless heart at ease. In fact, it led to an inner turmoil unlike anything he had ever experienced. It raised questions about his newly revealed father and his beliefs, and forced him to struggle within himself regarding his own beliefs and how he should live the rest of his life.

Anam thanked Eli and the other shepherds for their hospitality as he prepared for the long journey home. Samuel brought him a large sack containing food and other provisions to make his trip more comfortable. "You are too kind," Anam said. "I cannot repay you."

"Your smile and the knowledge that you will have a full stomach as you travel are thanks enough for me, friend," Samuel replied.

Eli embraced Anam. "Truly, your coming here was directed by God. Of that, I am quite certain."

"As am I," said Anam softly.

"Here," Eli handed Anam a large scroll, which had been rolled up and held tight by a silver clasp. "I want you to have this."

Taking it into his hands, Anam asked, "What is this?"

"A gift from your father. He gave it to me as his way of thanking me for coming to him first with the blessed news from the lips of the angel. It is something so special to me that I have hidden it away in my heart. Now it is time to pass it on to you."

"I cannot accept this. You said it was special to you. You mustn't …"

"Yes, but I no longer have need of the physical part of the gift. What is of the spirit will stay with me forever."

Anam did not fully understand Eli's words, but he would not dispute them further. He simply said, "Thank you," and with one final round of farewells, he was off.

Anam once again found himself back on the main road. To get home he would have to pass through Bethlehem again, though he had no intention of stopping this time. It suddenly came to him what Eli had said about the synagogue where his father was killed: that the ruins remained to this day.

Anam came upon a farmer repairing a fence on his property. He approached the middle-aged man. "Good sir, if you will, please direct me toward the ruins of the synagogue that stood in this town some thirty years ago."

The farmer looked at him suspiciously. "It was destroyed when I was a young child. It's just an old pile of rubble and ashes now. Why do you want to know where it is?"

"It is difficult to explain, but, please sir, I would be most grateful for your assistance."

After stroking his chin for a moment, the farmer shrugged. "Well, I suppose no harm can come from it." He directed Anam to a spot near the edge of some woods at the outer fringes of town. Anam thanked the man and went on his way.

As he walked toward the ruined sanctuary, Eli's words played over and over again in his mind. Anam's father Issachar had obviously been a very brave man. He died standing up for what he believed. But this faith that Issachar had in Jesus, what sense did it make? After all, this Jesus was a tiny baby. How could his father be so certain he would grow up to be the Messiah? A child could take many different kinds of paths in life. Anam couldn't imagine how his father could have such steadfast certitude that this boy would go on to greatness.

In fact, what reason was there to believe that he had survived at all? According to everyone he had spoken to, the soldiers killed all the male babies soon after Jesus' birth. Since it was Jesus whose life they sought, wouldn't it have made sense that they did indeed find and kill him? If that were so, then his father had died for nothing. He had been killed defending one who was already dead!

Anam turned off the main road where the helpful farmer had told him there would be an old overgrown side road that led to the ruins of the synagogue. Overhead birds went about their daily business, fluttering from one treetop to the next in the warm sunshine, oblivious to the feelings that were tearing this human being's heart asunder. He envied them sometimes. The lives of animals seemed so simple and carefree compared to the complex and often troubling ways of men.

His mind again turned to Jesus. Even if he did somehow survive the slaughter, what reason was there for Anam to believe he was truly the Messiah? Yes, this good man he now knew to be his father firmly believed Jesus was the Promised One of Israel, as did the shepherds. But that was many years ago, and nothing had been heard from Jesus or his family since, at least as far as Anam was aware. Was it possible that they were wrong? Could the townspeople of Bethlehem have been right after all? If so, then the gullibility of his father and the shepherds had led to all of the death and destruction. Maybe the shepherds' persistent faith only proved that they were stubborn old men who, out of guilt or pride or both, refused to admit they had been wrong. Then again, their belief seemed so pure.

Searching deep within his soul, Anam felt that every time he came close to a conclusion, doubts and new questions would begin his quest for answers all over again.

The path became more overgrown with weeds and seemed to be heading nowhere. Anam was getting hot and tired, and he began to think he should just forget this foolish idea and head directly for home. But then as he rounded a bend, he saw it. Laid out before him was a clearing, and as he drew closer he could see that the foundation of a large building was still there, though now it was just an enormous hole in the ground. Inside the hole were burnt slabs of wood, charred black and rotting from years of decay and exposure to the elements. "So this was your holy place, my father," Anam whispered as a light wind tousled his hair.

He walked closer to inspect the place in more detail. There was not much left of it. The charred remains of some furniture, perhaps benches where the congregation once sat for worship services, were scattered about, but there was not much more. Clearly, this was a place that mankind had turned its back on a long time ago. It seemed like the kind of lonely, deserted place that time itself had forgotten. Anam looked about and noticed that there weren't even any birds here, though they were plentiful less than a mile down the road. Both man and beast had apparently forsaken this place, he thought.

Near what he surmised was the entrance, he found a large boulder. He sat on it and closed his eyes. "Issachar, my father," he said into the whispering wind, "I know in my heart you were a good man. And I believe that you and Mother wanted only the best for me. But now I need your guidance. Is there any sign you can give me to lead me to the truth? Only the soft breeze replied.

Anam stood and stretched. As much as he wanted to stay and find out more about his past, this place was not providing any answers. Just as he was about to leave, the sack he had placed on the boulder fell off and tumbled to the ground. When he turned to pick it up, he noticed that the scroll Eli had given him had slipped out of the sack and the silver clasp that held it shut had come unhinged. He stooped down to pick it up, and his eye landed upon something in the writing that captured his attention.

In large, carefully drawn, almost delicate script were the words, "The Testimony of Issachar." Anam recognized the writing. It was the same as the writing on the lambskin blanket. The scroll was worn and soiled. It was apparent that Eli had read it many times. Anam felt a strong impulse to read. He sat back down on the boulder, gathered the scroll in his hands, and began.

His heart beat faster as he read the story that it told. Issachar was proclaiming that Jesus was the Messiah, and he was using the words of the prophets to demonstrate that Jesus was indeed the one of whom they had written. He had also recorded the testimonies of an assortment of people who had witnessed the extraordinary events surrounding the birth of Jesus. The evidence his father had amassed was remarkable.

The most compelling evidence came from the pages of Scripture. The parchment scroll included numerous references from the ancient books of the prophets. From the Book of Isaiah he read, *Therefore the Lord himself shall give you a sign; behold, a virgin shall conceive, and bear a son, and shall call his name Immanuel.* In all the accounts Issachar had heard from various witnesses, including that of a highly respected priest named Zacharias who was a close relative of Mary, there had never been any doubt that Mary the mother of Jesus was a virgin.

Anam was fascinated as he read about three powerful men, called magi, from distant lands who came to give homage to Jesus upon his birth. They came to Bethlehem following a bright new star that heralded this miraculous event. Isaiah had foretold their visit with incredible detail by saying: *Nations will come to your light, and kings to the brightness of your rising ... They will bring gold and frankincense, and will bear good news of the praises of the Lord.* Issachar had personally seen the gifts the magi had presented to Jesus, and they did, indeed, include gold and frankincense.

Remarkably, even the shepherds themselves were foretold in the ancient Scriptures. In the Book of Psalms, Issachar had noted the following: *They that dwell in the wilderness shall bow before him.*

Anam was especially startled to read the prophecy of Micah, for whom his surrogate father had been named. The following verse was inscribed upon the parchment: *But thou, Bethlehem Ephratah, though thou be little among the thousands of Judah, yet out of thee shall he come forth unto me that is to be ruler in Israel; whose goings forth have been from of old, from everlasting.*

This oracle had been written many centuries earlier, yet the accuracy of this prophecy was uncanny. Anam concluded that these signs, along with many others that Issachar had compiled and recorded, could point to none other than Jesus—the Messiah. He read for hours, for so long in fact that he lost track of the time.

At last Anam came to the end of his reading. He carefully rolled up the scroll and held it shut with the silver clasp. He kissed the coarse parchment before reverently placing it back inside the sack of provisions Samuel had given to him.

The weight of the evidence his father, Issachar the priest, had amassed attesting that Jesus was the Messiah left Anam with a profound respect for this man he had never known. "Yet your blood flows through my veins," he whispered.

His father had been a wise man indeed. He searched the word of God, and when the Messiah came, he was ready to welcome him. His faith in God and in the prophets was unshakable, and he paid for it with his life.

But what of me? Anam asked himself. *Now that I also know of this great truth, what shall I do with it? Do I remain silent, or was I, too, chosen to be a witness?* Unlike his father, Anam had never been in the presence of this Jesus, so perhaps his life had no great purpose. Now that he had learned the truth about his parents, maybe he should just go home, settle down with some nice peasant girl, and live out the remainder of his days.

Ready to move on again, Anam decided he would not leave Bethlehem before stopping to thank Johanan, the innkeeper who had been kind enough to tell him where he could meet the shepherds at their winter pasture. Micah had always taught him the importance of showing gratitude to those who help us, so the gesture only seemed fitting.

By the time he reached the inn, it was late in the afternoon and the sun was slowly descending on the horizon. He entered the inn and found Johanan looking much happier than when he had last visited. This time he sat at the dinner table with a strong-looking, matronly woman. Both of them turned when Anam entered the room.

"We have a visitor," said the woman.

Johanan broke into a wide smile. "Ah, I know this gentleman. My love, this is the man I told you about earlier."

Anam felt surprised. *Why would they be talking about me?* he wondered.

When Johanan insisted he have dinner with them, Anam sat at the table. The innkeeper introduced the woman as his wife, Raisa.

"When I was here two days ago," said Anam, "you were sick and unable to join your husband for the evening meal. I am glad to see that you are better now."

"Praise be to God," said Raisa. "I had been told there was no chance of recovery. We all thought this was a sickness unto death. My relatives had even prepared my burial plot. But in his goodness, the Lord sent us a healer, and now I feel like a healthy young girl."

This was remarkable. Prayers for the sick were always a part of sacred tradition, but Anam had never heard of such a miraculous healing. "That is indeed wonderful news. Please tell me how it came about."

Johanan looked Anam directly in the eye. "You may find this hard to believe, but earlier today a group of strangers came into Bethlehem. Their leader was a rabbi whose reputation as a miracle worker has been growing for some time.

Normally, I put no stock in such claims. Yet with my beloved Raisa so near to death, I felt I had no choice but to seek him out. I invited him into my house. And with the laying on of his hands, in an instant Raisa arose from her bed and was cured. This rabbi said to her, 'Your faith has healed you, woman.' It was absolutely amazing."

Johanan's next words were even more startling. "The man was the one they call Jesus."

A lump formed in Anam's throat. This was almost too much to bear. "Jesus, the very one whose name you refused to hear?"

Johanan confirmed it with a nod. "Yes, it was he. Jesus and some of his followers were passing through town, and he was showing them the place of his birth. I now realize that the massacre was not his fault. It happened due to the acts of evil men who were jealous of his power and wanted to kill him. But he survived their wicked plot and lived on into manhood to perform good deeds and preach salvation. This man, I now believe, truly has been sent by God to deliver his people."

Raisa said to Anam, "My husband was telling me that you have a lambskin inscribed with the words of an angel announcing the birth of Jesus. He seems to be connected to your own birth in some mysterious sort of way."

"Yes. Yes, I now believe that he is." Anam was thrilled to think that Jesus was so nearby. He felt as if his life would not be fulfilled if he did not find him. "I would like to meet this Jesus too. Where might I find him?"

The innkeeper explained that Jesus and his followers did not stay in Bethlehem very long. They left town quickly to avoid any trouble with the locals. This was clearly a man of peace who sought to avoid violence and strife.

Jesus had gone to show his disciples the stable where he was born. Then the group was going to find the shepherds at their winter pasture. "It's been only a few hours since they departed," the old man said. "If you hurry you might be able to catch up with them." Johanan told him of a shortcut through some rough country that would save him a significant amount of time.

Anam thanked the man and his wife for their hospitality. Then he set off down the road again, hoping to find out at last if everything he had come to believe was really true.

8
CHAPTER

ℐnam ran as fast as he could down a small, barely discernable path outside of town, arriving at the shepherds' encampment just as dusk enveloped the countryside. His arms and legs bore multiple scrapes from the thorns and branches that covered many sections of the rough trail. Yet he paid them no attention as he came upon Jonas, the young shepherd he'd first encountered upon his arrival the day before, cleaning up the remnants of the evening meal. "Jonas, my friend," he called out. "I am so glad to see you."

Jonas spun around. "Anam! We thought you had returned to your own town. Is something wrong?"

"No, nothing is wrong. I just need to know. Is he here yet?"

Jonas cocked his head. "Is *who* here?"

Anam then knew that Jesus and his friends must not have arrived yet. With the shortcut he took, he would be in time. "You'll see," he said, smiling. "Where is Eli?"

"Down at the stream with the others, washing up, and then to say the evening prayer. I am going to join them as soon as I finish here."

Anam helped him put away the cookware and utensils. "Jonas," he said, "I believe tonight all of our prayers will be answered."

They quickly completed their task and walked to the little stream to meet Eli and the other shepherds. All of them were astonished to see Anam back so soon, especially Eli. "Is something wrong, my son? Why have you not gone home?"

Before he could reply, Samuel pointed and said, "Look! Some men are coming down from that hilltop in the distance." Indeed, three strangers walked toward them down the hill. The setting sun behind them cast an unnatural glow around their silhouettes.

"Let's continue with our prayers, but keep a watchful eye as they approach," Eli warned. He turned to Anam. "Why don't you join us? We say this prayer every morning and evening … to remember what the angel said. I think you will recognize it."

The shepherds stood in a circle as they reverently recited words that had long been etched into their memories. "Glory to God in the highest heaven, and peace on earth to men of good will, through Jesus Christ, who was born of Mary in a stable in Bethlehem and who, wrapped in swaddling clothes, was in a manger, he who is the Savior of the world."

As they finished, the three strangers drew near to them.

All eyes turned to the newcomers, none of whom looked familiar. As the small band descended the hill, their leader, a tall, sturdy-looking man with longish brown hair, a thick beard, and piercing brown eyes, said, "Peace be with you, my friends."

The shepherds looked at the man suspiciously. After an awkward silence, Eli asked, "Who are you?"

The stranger smiled broadly. "One who loves you."

Eli seemed astounded by this curious reply. "Well, if that is so, you would be the first in many years."

The stranger stepped closer. His face had such a loving expression, the shepherds seemed to relax their guarded demeanor. "I am a rabbi. These two men are my disciples. I have come to show them my place of birth, and to find some long-lost friends."

"Then, you were born here near Bethlehem?" Eli inquired.

"Yes. During the time of the census. We lived in Bethlehem but a short time, and I wish to be reunited with some men who were my first friends, and who were a great help to my family during those days."

Anam could see that Eli was studying the stranger's face more intently. The man made a splendid appearance, though his mode of dress was humble. He did not look like any rabbi Anam had ever seen. Rabbis usually wore sumptuous, colorful robes lined with fringes. His dress was plain by comparison, yet he had a dignified manner about him. Also, rabbis were generally fat, living richly off the alms extracted from the faithful. This man was thin, muscular, and handsome.

The tall stranger never changed his smiling, loving expression. After a short pause, he spoke again. "I heard your prayer as we were approaching. It is a very unusual prayer. Where did you learn such a prayer?"

Eli, who was still staring at the stranger's radiant face, spoke up. "It is a prayer taught to us by an angel of the Lord long ago. On a cold night, the angel appeared, and the sky was as bright as day. The angel announced the birth of the Messiah in Bethlehem."

"Messiah? Is it this Jesus you mentioned in your prayer? Is he your Messiah?" The stranger was still smiling as he asked.

"Yes, my lord. His name is Jesus. But he is not just *our* Messiah. He was sent by God for the salvation of the whole world. We adored him as a newborn infant that night. Oh! He was so beautiful! And his mother … !"

"What happened to the child? Does he yet live?"

"I wish we knew. I heard he fled Bethlehem before Herod's slaughter, but we have had no word of him since. We have been persecuted and treated like murderers, but it would all be worth it if we only knew he is alive. Still, even if we never see him again, we will continue saying to everyone who will listen, 'The Messiah is born. The Savior is in the world. Angels told us so, and angels do not lie.'" Eli grew more animated as he spoke. "And so, every morning at sunrise and every evening when the first star appears, we repeat the angel's words as a prayer, and ask God to show us Jesus."

A tear appeared in the stranger's eye. He opened his arms as if to embrace the entire group. In a strong, loving voice, he said, "God has answered your prayer tonight. It is I, Jesus."

All the men fell to their knees. "You? Oh! Lord!" The old man kissed Jesus' feet as tears flowed freely down his face. The others knelt with their eyes wide and their mouths open. "I prayed I would live to see you again," Eli said. "Now, even if I die, I shall be content that I did not hope in vain."

"Please get up. Tell me your names. My mother spoke of you often. I wish to know you. I have come to stay with you, to share a meal with you, to comfort you, and to be your friend."

After a short reunion, Jesus led the men in prayer and introduced them to his two disciples, brothers named James and John. The group returned to the camp and lit a great bonfire, then sat and listened to every word Jesus had to say. "I want you men to know that I never forgot you. Though I was a mere babe when you came to offer me your adoration and gifts, my mother has many times recounted to me the story of your visit. She wishes you to know that, to this very day, she fondly recalls your kindness."

"It is we who are in her debt, Master," Eli said. "Those of us who were there recall the splendor of her grace. We were privileged to have been witnesses to the miraculous circumstances of your birth. Please tell me, if I should be so bold as to ask, why were we chosen for such an honor, and not the important men? We are but humble shepherds."

Jesus smiled upon him. He made eye contact with the two disciples he had brought with him. "There is a lesson here for all," he said to the entire group. "In my kingdom, greatness is not measured as it is by the standards of this world. Those who have labored righteously in humility shall be richly rewarded by my Father. And many whom this world considers great shall not be."

The disciple named John said to Eli, "We have heard that a great massacre took place here. The people of Bethlehem hold you in scorn and contempt, having blamed you for the tragedy."

Sitting quietly by Eli's side, Anam was taking in every word that was uttered. John's question went to the heart of the shepherds' dilemma, and Anam had now reached the point where he fully understood that they were blameless, yet continued to pay the price for an unjust accusation.

"It is true," Eli said to John. "But we are here to listen to the words of Jesus, not the sad memories of an old man."

At that, Jesus looked into Eli's eyes, his own piercing brown eyes full of compassion. "Do not speak ill of yourself, my friend. Your story is important to me. In fact, that was one of my reasons for coming here. My mother has told me many times how she wondered what became of you. Please tell me, so I, in turn, can tell her."

Anam could see that Eli was having a hard time continuing. He also noticed how patiently Jesus waited for the old man. Nothing in Jesus' demeanor seemed at all demanding, yet there was a sense about him that he was nonetheless in complete control. He was far different from anybody Anam had ever met before.

Finally, Eli collected himself and began to speak. "Your disciple is correct, Master, there was indeed a time of bloodshed and death. It seems your mother and Joseph had already fled with you, yet Herod and his minions were unaware. In their deadly quest, they searched high and low, and many met an untimely and cruel death at their wicked hands."

Eli wiped a tear from his eye. "The parents of those precious infants did all they could to protect them. Many were slain in their futile efforts to halt the killing. I had a wife and child of my own. I was not home when the soldiers came. They … they …"

"There is no need to continue," Jesus said. "I know the rest of the story. Your wife and son perished. You were not able to even bury them, as the people of the town cast stones at you and threatened your life."

Anam was amazed. Jesus seemed to know all about them even before they told him. Yet he had such tremendous compassion for them that he wanted to hear their own stories in their own words, to let them know how much he cared. Anam could not take his eyes off of him.

Fighting back tears, Eli said, "But I did not lose my faith in you. My fellow shepherds and I have gone all throughout the countryside and told all we have met what the angel told us. We have felt compelled to announce to all Israel that the Messiah has been born, and that a mighty angel of God has proclaimed it so. And we have done thus for these many years."

James then spoke up for the first time. "And how have they received your report? Do they believe?"

Eli shook his head. "Sadly, most do not. In fact, because of the massacre, and the fact that we are the ones who first proclaimed Jesus as the Messiah, they have treated us as evildoers and outcasts. We have been hated and despised ever since."

Jesus turned his head slowly until he had looked each of the shepherds directly in the eye. "You have suffered greatly all these years for the sake of the truth. Though it may seem that your efforts have been in vain, they have not. For you have planted seeds among the people, preparing the way for the appearance of the Son of Man. Many will taste of salvation thanks to the bitter cup all of you have swallowed."

Anam sensed that these words of Jesus were like the Balm of Gilead for the souls of these faithful men who had dedicated their lives to spreading the message they had received from God delivered by his angel. Almost as if on cue, the assembled group hailed Jesus with a mighty shout: "Praise be to God!" They had at last been vindicated.

Jesus spoke to the shepherds, individually and in small groups, late into the night. He answered their questions and filled their hearts with God's love and the promise of his future kingdom.

At last all the men returned to their tents, singing songs of praise and celebrating this momentous event. For the older shepherds, this was their second encounter with Jesus, having been with him thirty years prior as a newborn in that cold yet magical stable, and throughout his stay in Bethlehem.

For the younger ones, after hearing about him all their lives, this was the first time they were actually in the Messiah's presence. But for all of them, it was an evening that would change their lives forever. He had touched them like the rays of the sun touching the earth on a warm spring morning.

Anam remained alone with Jesus. He had much to say, but he was so in awe of this man that he could not speak.

"You have come here for a reason, Anam," Jesus said. He had phrased it like a question, but to Anam's ears it sounded like a statement. And he knew that Jesus was right.

"Yes, Rabbi," he said. "I came here to find out who I am. I did not know my name or my heritage, but now I do."

Jesus looked deep into Anam's eyes. "Yet your heart still is not at ease. You came seeking flesh and blood answers, and that is what you have found."

He was right. Anam felt as if there was still a piece of the puzzle missing. "My entire life I wanted to know my name, and I thought when I discovered it I would know my purpose in life. But, alas, I am still adrift and without direction."

"The kingdom you have heard me speak about tonight is not of this world. It is of the world to come. It is a great banquet to which all shall be called, though not everyone will answer the call."

Anam understood the implications of his words. "Have I been called?"

"You have said it with your own lips."

"Am I to become your follower?"

"Is this what you believe, Stephen?"

This was the first time Anam had heard anyone call him by what he now knew was his rightful name. Without hesitation he replied, "My father searched the Scriptures and died for his belief in you, and the prophets of old foresaw your coming. Yes, I believe that you are the promised Messiah. But I do not know if I am worthy to follow you. I am a person of such little value."

Jesus smiled and reached out to touch Anam's head. "Stephen, it is for such as you that I have come. You have come to know the life of the outcast, and your heart identifies with those who are in pain. You shall indeed follow me, and your deeds will earn you a special place in paradise, along with your father."

Anam marveled at these words. For the first time, he felt as if he had a God-given purpose and mission for his life.

The next day, soon after rising, James and John told the shepherds that their visit must come to an end. Jesus was prepared to move on. Eli spoke for the entire group as they gathered to say farewell. "We cannot bear to have you leave us, Master. We beseech you, please let us come with you and serve you."

"Nay, it is not possible to come with me. You must go in the opposite direction, where you will serve me still. There is much territory to be covered, and the good news must be spread throughout all Israel."

"But we are not learned men, Master. We must be taught by you before we can go out into the world."

But Jesus said, "Even before I came to visit you, all of you shepherds were steadfastly doing my Father's work. You have spoken the truth of what the angel said to you, even when others cursed you and persecuted you. Go now, and continue to proclaim the truth, and let all who have ears hear it."

Anam approached Jesus. "Master," he said, gesturing to the assembled shepherds, "What will happen to these men? They have already suffered for so long. Now that you are here, must they continue to suffer?"

Jesus fixed his gaze upon Anam. "Many will suffer because of me. Indeed, some will give their lives for my sake. And great will be their reward in heaven."

He turned to the shepherds. "In those times of suffering and persecution, remember the newborn infant you adored on that night long ago, and I will come to you. Do not weep. I will not leave you alone. Your kindness wiped my tears when I was crying in the manger. Is my kindness not sufficient to wipe yours? In this world there will always be hatred and violence and suffering. But let not your hearts be troubled. Let my peace protect and comfort you."

Jesus embraced each of the men. "What you saw that night in the stable in Bethlehem was the unfolding of God's plan to reconcile men to himself. All will come to its fulfillment in God's perfect timing. It was with good reason that my Father in heaven chose a lowly stable as the place of my birth. It was to confound the wise of this world. They look to rich men and palaces, but God is not impressed with these. Yea, I tell you, all of the wealth and power of this world is as nothing to him who resides in heaven. Creator of all that is, he asks only one thing of those whom he calls his children: that they love him without reservation and accept the gift of his love as he freely pours it out unto them.

"Continue spreading the word of truth you have received. Go and light the fire of God in the hearts of men.

"Good-bye, my friends. Remain steadfast in your faith in God and in the one sent by him to deliver the world unto salvation. I shall return to you soon."

Without further conversation he blessed them, and they watched with great joy in their hearts as he and his disciples journeyed forth.

A WORD FROM THE AUTHOR

The Bible tells us that the shepherds of Bethlehem were the first to hear about the miraculous birth of the Savior, Jesus Christ. This momentous and joyful occasion was, sadly, followed by the slaughter of innocent children by the jealous and cruel King Herod. In all likelihood, these events profoundly influenced these simple men and remained with them for the rest of their lives.

The character of Anam was inspired by the historical figure known as Stephen. He was one of the earliest followers of Jesus, and, in fact, the first Christian martyr. His story is told in the Bible (Acts 6-7).

Here is the section from the Bible on the death of Stephen. It begins with Stephen castigating the Pharisees, the religious leaders who orchestrated Jesus' crucifixion.

"You stubborn people! You are heathen at heart and deaf to the truth. Must you forever resist the Holy Spirit? But your ancestors did, and so do you! Name one prophet your ancestors didn't persecute! They even killed the ones who predicted the coming of the Righteous One— the Messiah whom you betrayed and murdered. You deliberately disobeyed God's law, though you received it from the hands of angels.

The Jewish leaders were infuriated by Stephen's accusation, and they shook their fists in rage. But Stephen, full of the Holy Spirit, gazed steadily upward into heaven and saw the glory of God, and he saw Jesus standing in the place of honor at God's right hand. And he told them, "Look, I see the heavens opened and the Son of Man standing in the place of honor at God's right hand!"

Then they put their hands over their ears, and drowning out his voice with their shouts, they rushed at him. They dragged him out of the city and began to stone him. The official witnesses took off their coats and laid them at the feet of a young man named Saul.

And as they stoned him, Stephen prayed, "Lord Jesus, receive my spirit." And he fell to his knees, shouting, "Lord, don't charge them with this sin!" And with that, he died.

Both Stephen and the Bethlehem shepherds epitomize the earliest Christian believers. Their unwavering faith, even in the face of barbaric persecution, helped build up the early church as it sought to spread the message of Jesus to the world. My prayer is for all who follow Christ to draw inspiration from those first believers. They lived their lives as humble yet heroic champions of the faith, and their witness remains as powerful today as it was two thousand years ago.

ABOUT THE AUTHOR

RICHARD M. BARRY, an author, publisher, inventor, entrepreneur and committed Christian, wrote *The Shepherds' Prayer* to help disseminate the untold story of the Bethlehem shepherds of the Bible. A labor of love, the inspiring story of tragedy, suffering, faith, hope and triumphant vindication took nine years to complete.

A native of Texas, Richard now lives with his family in Centennial, Colorado.

More information about The Shepherds' Prayer is on the Internet at www.ShepherdsPrayer.com. Please tell us about your experience reading the book. We welcome your comments.

THE
SHEPHERDS'
PRAYER

A Christmas Novel

If you have enjoyed this book, maybe the people on your Christmas list will enjoy receiving it as a gift. It is also available as an audiobook, narrated by veteran actor, John McDonough. Generous discounts are available for orders of five or more books.

Telephone 1-888-209-0510

Or visit www.ShepherdsPrayer.com